I AM READING

PURR-FECT PETE

SAMANTHA HAY

ILLUSTRATED BY

CHRIS INNS

KINGFISHER
NEW YORK

For Alice and Archie—S. H.
For Fiona, a spectacular act—C. I.

Text copyright © 2008 by Samantha Hay
Illustrations copyright © 2008 by Chris Inns
KINGFISHER
Published in the United States by Kingfisher, an imprint of Henry Holt and Company LLC,
175 Fifth Avenue, New York, New York, 10010. First published in Great Britain by Kingfisher
Publications plc, an imprint of Macmillan Children's Books, London.

Distributed in Canada by H. B. Fenn and Company Ltd.

Library of Congress Cataloging-in-Publication Data
has been applied for.

ISBN: 978-0-7534-6242-3

Kingfisher books are available for special promotions and premiums.
For details contact: Director of Special Markets, Holtzbrinck Publishers.

First American Edition May 2008
Printed in China
1TR/1207/WKT/SC(SC)/IISMA/C

Contents

Chapter One

When High-Wire Wilma fell and broke her tail, everyone said that the Flying Fur Balls were finished!

The Flying Fur Balls
were the best
acro-cats in
the world.
And Wilma
was the star
of their show.

Wilma was as brave as a lion.

She was as light as a kitten.

She could leap and twirl.
Tumble and whirl.

Backflip . . .

. . . body whip

. . . and balance on
absolutely anything.

But one night it all went wrong.

Wilma wobbled.

She was walking

on the wire when

she tripped

and fumbled.

Then tumbled . . .

. . . and crashed

to the ground.

Wilma quit!

"It's no use," she told the rest of the Flying Fur Balls. "I've used up eight of my nine lives. It's time to hang up my leotard!"

The Flying Fur Balls were shocked!

"But what about us?" they cried.

"We can't do acro-catics with only

four of us!"

Wilma shrugged.

"You'll need to look for a new member!"

Chapter Two

So they did.

The Flying Fur Balls

held an audition.

And every acro-cat

in the land came along.

"The cat we choose will need to be tough!" growled Gloria, the strongest of the Fur Balls. Gloria had the strength of ten cats and was always at the bottom of the acro-cat towers, which was just as well, because Gloria liked to eat salami sandwiches and had the most awful breath.

"The cat we choose will need to be small and springy," said Chin and Chen, who were terrific tumblers.

"And as brave as a lion!" said Brenda, who was a super stilt walker.

But the trouble was, they couldn't find any cat who measured up. "We might as well pack up and go home!" said Brenda as the last would-be Fur Ball was sent away with his tail between his legs. Then suddenly there was a pattering of tiny feet and the smell of stinky cheese . . .

The door crashed open, and there
stood a very small kitten.

Brenda put on her glasses. "I don't
think you're old enough to audition."

The tiny cat didn't
answer. Instead, he
did a handstand.

"Not bad," said
Chin and Chen.
"But do you have a spring in your step?"

The tiny cat leaped
in the air and
somersaulted
twice before
landing.

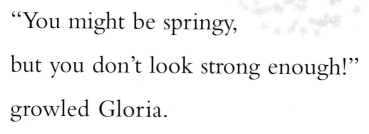

"You might be springy,
but you don't look strong enough!"
growled Gloria.

The tiny cat cartwheeled over, scooped
up Gloria, and twirled her above his head.
Then he backflipped onto the set of wall
bars, scrambled to the top, and dangled
Gloria down by her tail.
"You're hired!" they all shouted together.

Chapter Three

The tiny cat was named Pete.

He was as brave as
a lion and as light
as a kitten.

He could leap
and twirl.

Tumble and whirl.

Backflip . . .

. . . body whip

. . . and balance on
absolutely anything.

He fitted in
purr-fectly!

When Brenda did her amazing stilt-walking, plate-spinning spectacular, Pete stood on her shoulders spinning cups of cream.

When Chin and Chen did their world-famous supersonic tornado tumbles, Pete joined in, too, cartwheeling wildly until the audience felt dizzy watching him.

And when Gloria whizzed around the
ring on her motorcycle, driving it with
her toes, Pete stood on her head and
juggled milk bottles!

The Flying Fur Balls were a sellout.
And everyone agreed that Pete was
purr-fect!
Well . . . except for some quite
peculiar habits.

He never
ate fish.

He hated
cream.

And he liked to snack on stinky cheese.
And strangely, he didn't know any
good mouse jokes.
But the Flying Fur Balls didn't mind,
until one terrible night . . .

Chapter Four

It had been Pete's idea.

"I know," he'd suddenly squeaked
during rehearsal. "Why don't we try
something really spectacular? Why not
fire me out of a cannon, right up onto
the high wire—without a safety net?"

Brenda's
eyes popped.

Chin and
Chen gulped.

Gloria gasped.
It was the most
daring idea ever.

And they all agreed to try it out
that night . . .
The big top was full. Hundreds of
cats were packed in like sardines
to see the show.
"Ladies and
gentlemen!"
boomed Brenda,
standing on top
of the cannon.

"Tonight—Fur Ball Pete will attempt
the bravest feat . . ."
Pete took a bow.
"He'll cannonball onto the high wire
without a safety net!"
The audience gasped as Pete climbed
inside the cannon. Brenda lit the fuse.

There was a big bang . . .

a flash of orange . . .

and Pete shot out of the cannon like

a giant cork bursting out of a bottle.

Amazingly, he landed
right on target,
in the middle of the high wire.
The audience went crazy—meowing
and yowling and tossing their boxes
of tuna-fish popcorn into the air
with delight.

Fur Balls!

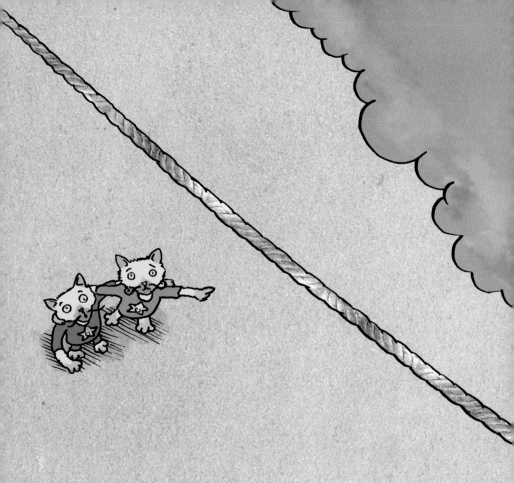

Pete, now balancing on the high wire, beamed and waved and didn't wobble even slightly.

But then Chin sniffed.

"What's that burning smell?"

Chen looked at Pete and gasped,

"He's on fire!"

Pete certainly was.

His fur had started to smoke when

he'd been shot out of the cannon.

Now it was covered in flames!

It looked like the end for Pete . . .

But it wasn't.

He suddenly did a very peculiar thing.

He grabbed his fur, zipped open

his belly, and then took off

all of his skin!

"Frozen fish bones!" gasped Gloria.

"Pete's a mouse!"

Chapter Five

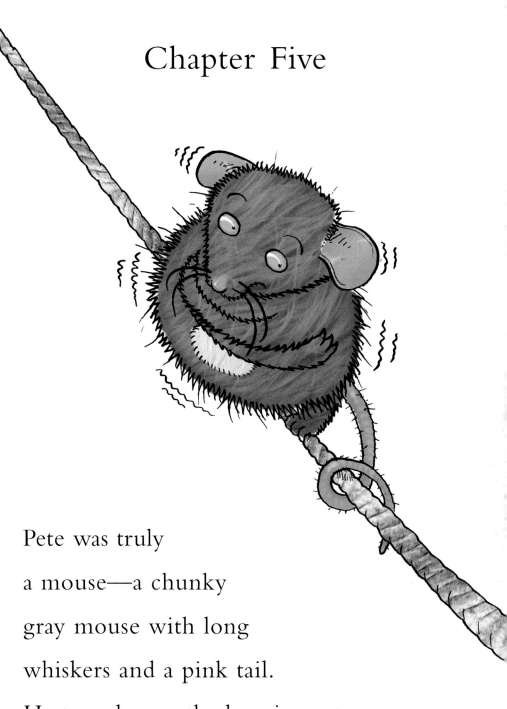

Pete was truly
a mouse—a chunky
gray mouse with long
whiskers and a pink tail.
He tossed away the burning cat
costume and stood shivering on the high wire.

Everyone was shocked and stunned.

Then suddenly a yowl from the

audience went up:

"EAT HIM!"

Pete peered down helplessly

at the angry cats.

Then something whizzed

past his ears.

It was a box of

tuna-fish popcorn.

The audience members

had started throwing

their show snacks at him!

Another box narrowly

missed him . . .

And then . . .

Thwack!

One hit him straight

on the head, and Pete

wobbled . . . and fumbled . . .

and tumbled.

"Ahhhhh!" he squeaked as he

crashed down toward the ground.

He covered his eyes and waited for

the splat. But it never came.

Just as he was about
to hit the ground, a
giant pair of paws
reached up and
caught him.
Pete gasped.
It was Gloria.
"P-p-p-p-please
don't eat me,"
he squeaked, smelling
her hot salami breath.

Chapter Six

But Gloria didn't eat Pete. Instead, she turned to the yowling audience and let out a loud growl.

"Listen, everyone! This mouse is the best acro-cat I've ever worked with."

"He may not actually be a cat," she added, "but I think Pete is pu**rr**-fect!"

The audience started spitting and hissing.

Gloria glowered at them. "And if any of you would like to eat Pete—you'll have to eat me first!"

The hissing and spitting stopped.

"And us, too," yowled Chin and Chen.

Brenda sighed. "And me, too, I suppose," she said.

The audience shuffled uncomfortably.

"Okay," Gloria said, "let's get on
with the show."
And amazingly, the Flying Fur Balls and
Pete carried on with their performance.

Much later, when the show was over
and the Fur Balls were back in their
dressing rooms, Pete apologized.
"I didn't mean to trick you," he
squeaked. "But I've always wanted
to be a Flying Fur Ball!"
Gloria shrugged. "But now that
everyone knows you're a mouse, you'll
have to leave. You won't want to end
up being someone's show snack!"
Pete nodded sadly.

But Brenda smiled and said, "Not so fast.
I have a plan."

The next day the Flying Fur Balls
announced Pete's retirement.
Then they secretly took him to a
costume shop and bought him
a new cat costume.

And a few days later, the Fur Balls announced the arrival of a new member of their troop: a kitten named Pedro.

Pedro looked a lot like Pete.

He was the same size and shape.

He didn't like fish or cream and he didn't know any good mouse jokes.

And he was always snacking on stinky cheese.

But unlike Pete, he never,
NOT EVER, not for all the stinky
cheese in the world, suggested that he
should climb inside a cannon and be
fired onto the high wire!

About the author and illustrator

Samantha Hay
worked in television
for ten years before
leaving to start a family
and write children's books.
Sam lives in Scotland and is
the author of *Creepy Customers*
and *Hocus-Pocus Hound*, other titles
in the *I Am Reading* series. "Even if I could find a cat
costume big enough, I don't think I'd be brave enough to
follow Pete onto the high wire. I'd be much happier being
Gloria—standing at the bottom of the Fur Ball towers."

Chris Inns is an exciting author
and illustrator of novelty and
picture books. Chris lives in
Kent, England, with his wife
and two young children.
"My cat Lizzie is far too lazy
to be one of the Flying Fur
Balls," says Chris, "but I
know she would like to be
in the audience eating
tuna-fish popcorn!"

Strategies for Independent Readers

Predict

Think about the cover, illustrations, and the title
of the book. What do you think this book will be about?
While you are reading think about what may
happen next and why.

Monitor

As you read ask yourself if what you're reading makes sense.
If it doesn't, reread, look at the illustrations, or read ahead.

Question

Ask yourself questions about important ideas
in the story such as what the characters might
do or what you might learn.

Phonics

If there is a word that you do not know, look carefully
at the letters, sounds, and word parts that you do know.
Blend the sounds to read the word. Ask yourself if this is
a word you know. Does it make sense in the sentence?

Summarize

Think about the characters, the setting where the
story takes place, and the problem the characters faced
in the story. Tell the important ideas in the beginning,
middle, and end of the story.

Evaluate

Ask yourself questions like: Did you like the story?
Why or why not? How did the author make the story
come alive? How did the author make the story fun to
read? How well did you understand the story? Maybe
you can understand it better if you read it again!